The Little Girl with Painted Hands

LorriMarie Jenkins

Written and Illustrated by LorriMarie Jenkins

AuthorHouse™
1663 Liberty Drive
Bloomington, IN 47403
www.authorhouse.com
Phone: 833-262-8899

This book is printed on acid-free paper.

ISBN: 978-1-6655-1731-7 (sc)
ISBN: 978-1-6655-1732-4 (e)

Library of Congress Control Number: 2021903311

Print information available on the last page.

Published by AuthorHouse 02/25/2021

author HOUSE

The Little Girl with Painted Hands

LorriMarie Jenkins

today I am going to tell you a story about a little girl...
a little girl that wanted very badly to fit in...
a little girl that was filled with fear about
being rejected for being 'different'...
a little girl that felt lonely even when she was
surrounded by groups of people.

once upon a time…. a long time ago…
a little baby girl was born into a small village.
everyone was so excited when the little girl was born…
they gathered around to sing her songs and to
welcome her into the village. everything
seemed normal…almost.

as the little girl grew...
she noticed that she had
something that no one else in
the village seemed to have...
she had paint on her hands...
beautiful paint...
blue, red, yellow...
and as she got older...
the colors of the paint
grew brighter.

One day, the little girl showed her mother the beautiful paint on her hands... her mother rushed the little girl to the river and scrubbed the little girls hands in the water... she scrubbed and scrubbed and scrubbed but the paint would not come off.

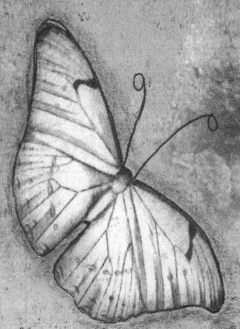

her mother was filled with
fear because she knew
if the other people in the village
saw that the little girl was different,
they would cast her out of the
village. only people with clean
hands could live in this village.

remember nothing
hall be glad to have moth
house is very damp.   It's a
be out, though !''
She *must* go !'' said Evesham.
I'll be back in half an hour—
shall not go,'' Dorothy said ;
st stay and look after the sto
hat's that ?''   Evesham   w
of water outside the d
's from the kitche

making
She ought to
e way of the w
ll always on
We'll t

ey started,
mother's spect
ays lay in a bo
m took her ge
across the

lane
arm-bui
Fixin' u
ain com
on, an
ncle

thee'd
preserved from
nd Barton ge
o stayed my
while h

dy

con

ned

the smok
ge of green,
the rain the ca
on sat in the
rness.   Th
eased

gh

A

the little girl became fearful too....
she did not want to have to leave the
village...she started to hide her hands.

manage the
...orting and kicking
...ions. In short, both in
...of it, nothing was thought
...f the removal of the capital
...oudest of the agitators was
...hat he cared one straw whether
...Fastburg, or to Slowburg
...for the money which he in
...agitation he did care
...ney he labored wi
...world alone.

she would not play with the other children... she was too afraid they would see her painted hands...she thrust her hands deep into her pockets and kept her eyes cast down...she was afraid and... she was different.

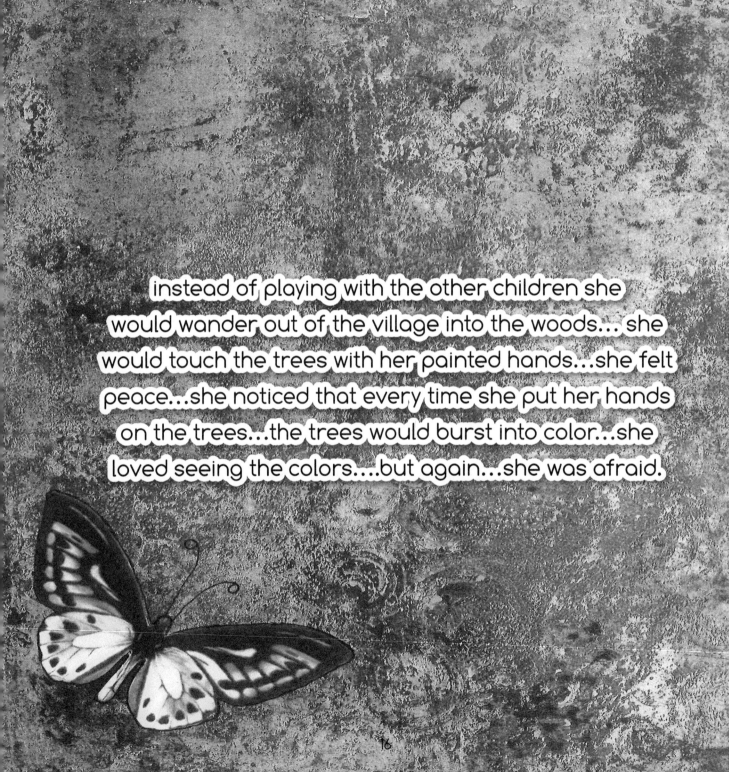

instead of playing with the other children she would wander out of the village into the woods... she would touch the trees with her painted hands...she felt peace...she noticed that every time she put her hands on the trees...the trees would burst into color...she loved seeing the colors....but again...she was afraid.

one day she wandered deeper into the woods... afraid that someone from the village would notice her painted hands... she was brushing her hands against the leaves...the rocks... the trees...even the birds that had become her friends... everything was bursting with color...she heard a noise.

she stopped touching things and quickly hid her hands in her pockets...out from behind one of the trees she could see a young boy...about her age... followed by a small group of people...they were all waving their hands proudly... proudly! they were waving their painted hands proudly!

the boy approached the little girl and said something that she did not understand...a language that she had never heard before... the boy held his hands close over his heart...as if protecting something...

the young boy was telling her that if she was brave enough to touch other people with her painted hands...that she would give the gift of courage to others....for the gift of painted hands is a gift to be shared...that once she was brave enough to share that gift...she would never feel lonely again....that her heart would soar with joy and gratitude.

as the young boy got closer to the little girl with painted hands... he removed his hands from his heart and extended them to her... the little girl could feel the joy that was in his hands...the life, the breath, and yes...the creativity.....

26

she put her painted hands in his painted hands
and instantly understood his language...he was telling her
to be proud of her painted hands...to protect her painted
hands from those that did not understand how powerful
her painted hands were...to bravely share her painted
hands with others that were still hiding their painted hands.

so i encourage you to be
brave....to wave your
painted hands proudly...to touch as
many people as you can...for you have
been given a gift....a responsibility...
the responsibility to find others with
painted hands that are still hiding
them deeply in their pockets.

be kind to yourself embrace your 'painted hands' and...
go create, go play, go have fun!
lorrimarie jenkins
(the little girl with painted hands)

The Little Girl with Painted Hands
written and illustrated by
LorriMarie Jenkins

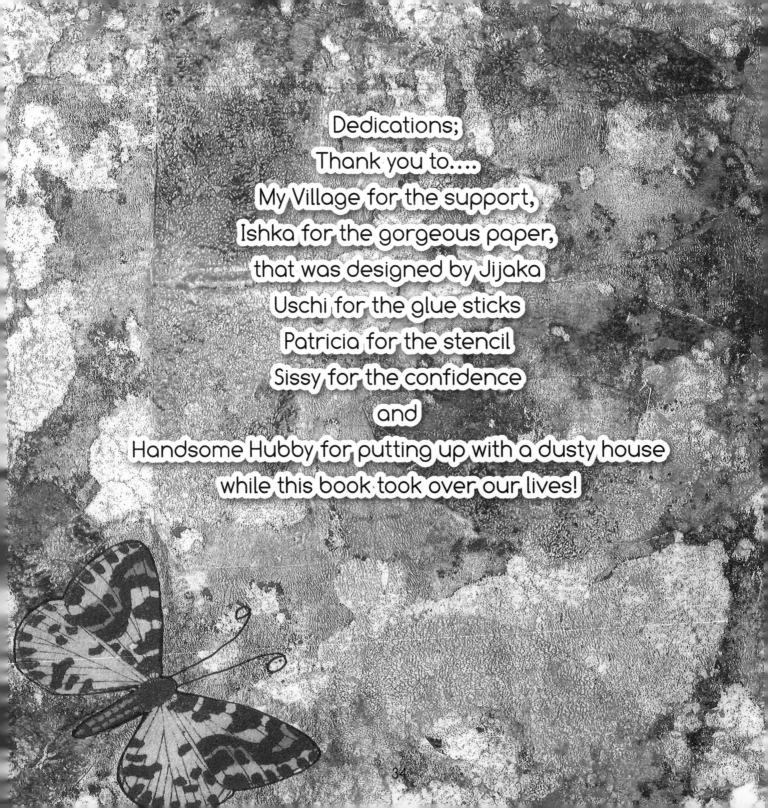

Dedications;
Thank you to....
My Village for the support,
Ishka for the gorgeous paper,
that was designed by Jijaka
Uschi for the glue sticks
Patricia for the stencil
Sissy for the confidence
and
Handsome Hubby for putting up with a dusty house
while this book took over our lives!

LorriMarie is a mixed media artist living in California with her Handsome Hubby Rob. She is a wife, a mother, a grandmother, a sister, a teacher, a mentor and a friend to many. She creates art on a daily basis and remains grateful that 'art is the universal language'. LorriMarie has a YouTube channel with over 500 mixed media videos and has over 30,000 subscribers in her 'Village'. She encourages others to 'use what they have' to create their art, to leave perfection outside the door and... to wave their painted hands proudly! and yes....'go create, go play, go have fun' is her favorite phrase.

CPSIA information can be obtained
at www.ICGtesting.com
Printed in the USA
LVHW072236170321
681810LV00009B/609

9 781665 517317